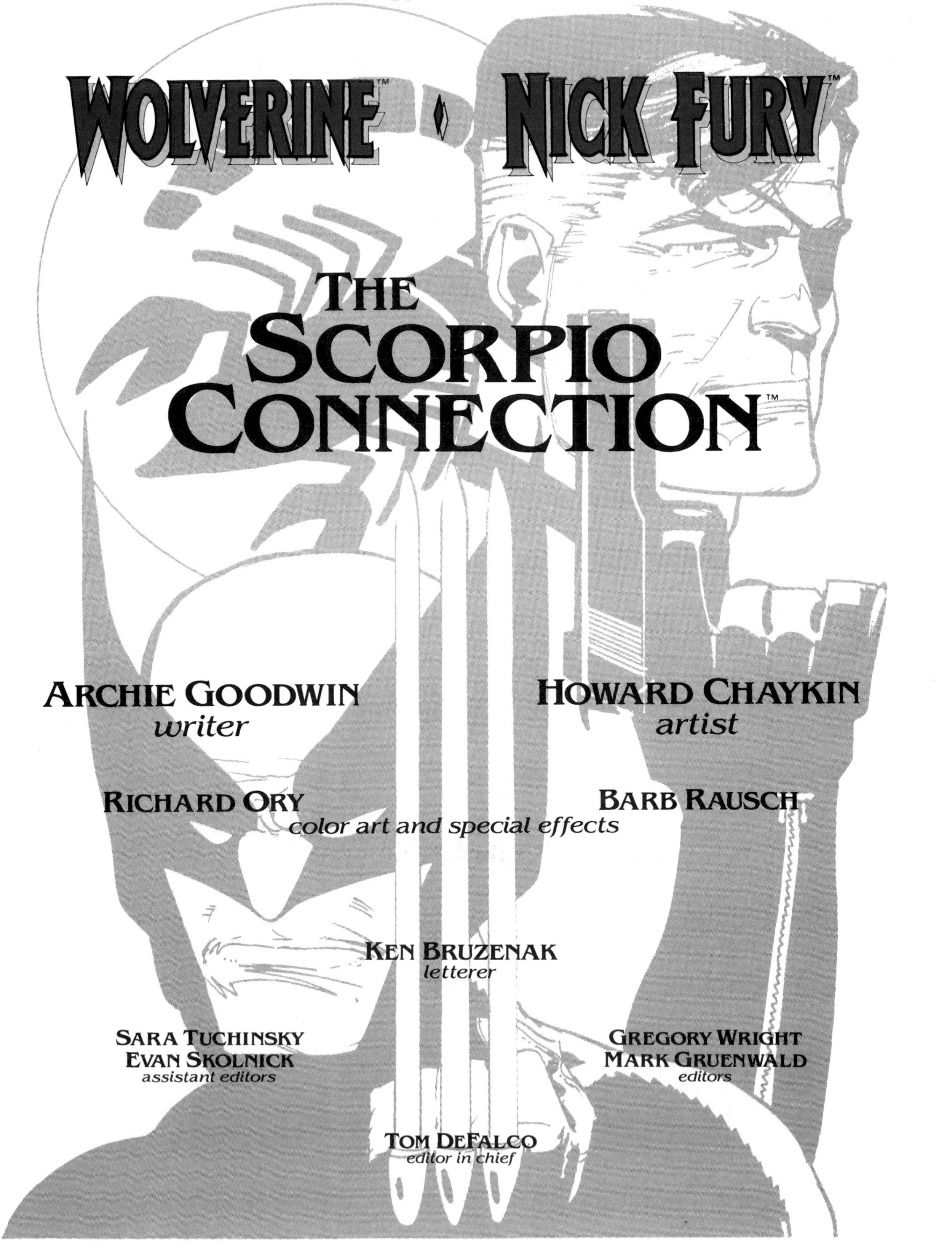

MARVEL® COMICS PRESENTS

# WOLVERINE™ ◆ NICK FURY™

# THE SCORPIO CONNECTION™

**ARCHIE GOODWIN**
*writer*

**HOWARD CHAYKIN**
*artist*

**RICHARD ORY**

**BARB RAUSCH**

*color art and special effects*

**KEN BRUZENAK**
*letterer*

**SARA TUCHINSKY**
**EVAN SKOLNICK**
*assistant editors*

**GREGORY WRIGHT**
**MARK GRUENWALD**
*editors*

**TOM DEFALCO**
*editor in chief*

### ACKNOWLEDGEMENT:
### TO
### JIM STERANKO
*creator of the original Scorpio*

DREAMTIME, DAVID NANJIWARRA THOUGHT AS HE BEGAN THE FINAL TEN MINUTES OF HIS LIFE.

DREAMTIME. THE WAY OLD TRIBESMEN BACK IN ARNHEM LAND RECKONED ANYTHING THEY OR SOMEONE THEY KNEW, HAD NEVER DIRECTLY EXPERIENCED.

DREAMTIME. NOT A BAD WAY TO CONSIDER HIS OWN LIFE SINCE LEAVING AUSTRALIA. LONG DAMN YEARS IN A FRUSTRATING DAMN BUSINESS.

THE BUSINESS OF BEING A SPY.

AND HERE, TWO THOUSAND FEET ABOVE THE URUBAMBA RIVER, AMID THE INCAN RUINS OF MACHU PICCHU, HIS PART IN THAT BUSINESS WAS ALMOST DONE.

UNDER COVER AS A VISITING ARCHEOLOGICAL TEAM, THE *SHIELD* ANTI-TERRORIST UNIT HAD BEEN IN PERU JUST OVER A WEEK. EIGHT NEGATIVE REPORTS FILED TO HEADQUARTERS IN THE STATES.

ORDERS TO PACK IT IN WOULDN'T BE MUCH LONGER COMING DOWN.

NANJIWARRA WOULD BE PACKING IT IN AS WELL. NO ONE WOULD BE SURPRISED. NOT AFTER ONE MORE DEAD END OPERATION, LATEST IN A STRING OF HARD LUCK FOR A MAN WHO WAS PLAGUED WITH IT.

WELL THEN, LARS--

--ANY *MIRACLES* IN SIGHT FOR US THIS MORNING?

THAT POT OF *COFFEE.* STUFF'S ACTUALLY DRINKABLE TODAY. AND I'VE BEEN THINKING, DAVID--

--SECTOR KILO-NINER, I SEE YOU DID PRELIMINARY RECON, PERHAPS A FOLLOW-UP WOULD--

SUNUVVA BITCH!

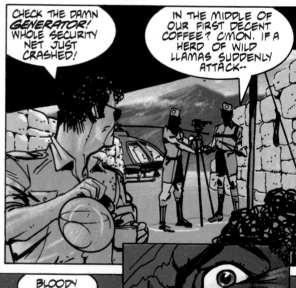

CHECK THE DAMN *GENERATOR!* WHOLE SECURITY NET JUST CRASHED!

IN THE MIDDLE OF OUR FIRST DECENT COFFEE? C'MON. IF A HERD OF WILD LLAMAS SUDDENLY ATTACK--

OUR *LOOKOUTS* CAN FINALLY EARN THEIR-- *AAGH!*

BLOODY HELL!

EVERY-BODY--

IT WASN'T GUNFIRE. IT WAS TOO FAST, TOO ACCURATE, TOO POWERFUL.

"DOWN!"

SOME *HIGHER* TECHNOLOGY HAD JUST RENDERED THE *SHIELD* OPERATION DEAD AS THE RUINS SURROUNDING IT.

ONE MAN. HAS TO BE. FROM THE SWEEP, THE DIRECTION OF FIRE. ONE MAN. DONE FOR US RIGHT AND PROPER—

--ONLY HE'S GOT TO COME AND MAKE *CERTAIN*, JUST....ABOUT...

NOW!

WHOEVER YOU ARE, WHILE YOUR HEAD'S RINGING FROM THAT--

--I'M GOING TO BE *BEHIND* YOU! THE NANJIWARRA HARD LUCK *ENDS*--

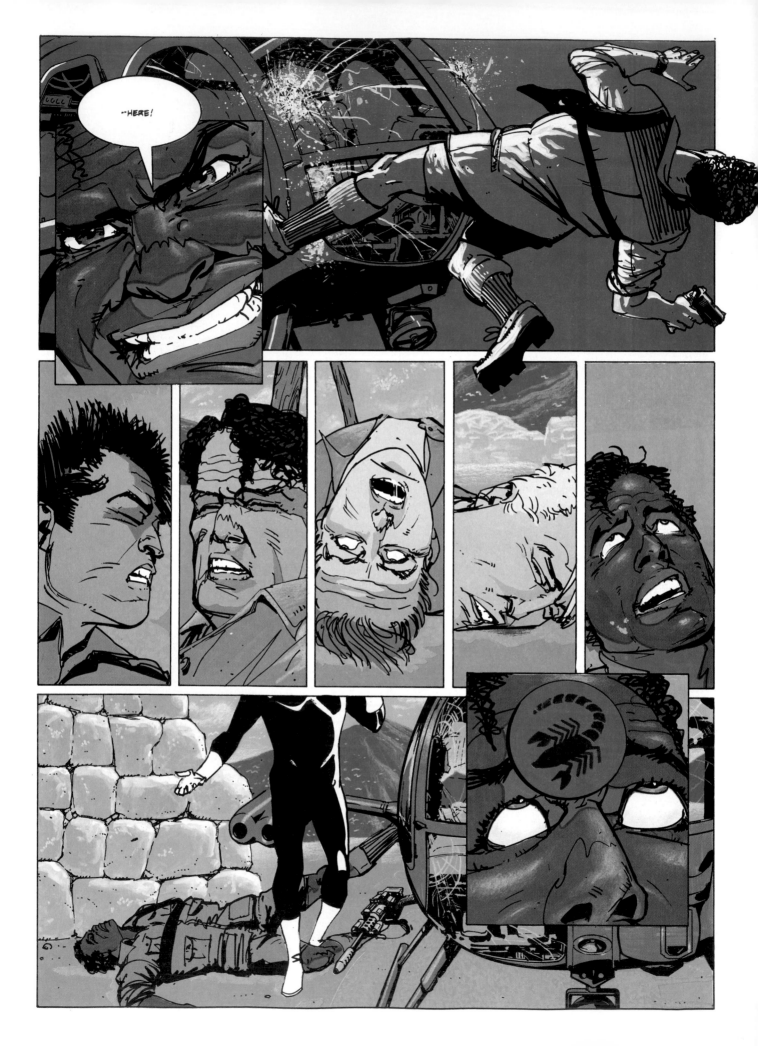

...AS ITS UNIQUELY EXCLUSIVE CLIENTELE. THE SHABBILY ELEGANT OLD BUILDING HAD RECENTLY BECOME, THROUGH AN IMPENETRABLE MAZE OF PROXY CORPORATIONS...

...THE PROPERTY OF THE INTERNATIONAL ESPIONAGE ORGANIZATION KNOWN BY ITS ACRONYM, **SHIELD** (SUPREME HEADQUARTERS INTERNATIONAL ESPIONAGE LAW-ENFORCEMENT DIVISION).

I'M NOT TALKING LIFETIME COMMITMENT, VAL, JUST *CASUAL*, YOU KNOW? CAB TO COLUMBUS AVENUE FOR A LITTLE FETTUCINI ALFREDO?

I MEAN, PART OF THE REASON FOR THE FACILITY *BEING* HERE IS SOCIAL, RIGHT...? MAKE THE EXERCISE PROGRAM MORE PLEASANT...REMOVE IT FROM NORMAL WORK PATTERNS...?

THAT'S THIS YEAR'S *THEORY*, AGENT CROSS..

--BUT MY ANSWER'S STILL *NO*. WHEN SAVING THE WORLD IS THE COMPANY BUSINESS... ANY OFFICE ROMANCE SOONER OR LATER GETS *DUMPED* FOR IT.

NATURE OF THE BEAST. BUT KNOWING THAT DOESN'T MAKE ME *HURT* LESS--

--AND, WITH ALL THE THINGS I'M GOOD AT, *CASUAL* WAS NEVER ONE OF THEM. SORRY, CROSS..

WE'RE *GOIN'* FOR IT! WE'RE *DOIN'* IT!

COM'N! COM'N!

WE'RE PUMPED! WE'RE PUSHIN'!

WE'RE GETTIN' IT ALL THE WAY! WE'RE BRINGIN' IT HOME!

D-DUGAN...

WHAT'S... THIS...WE... CRAP...?

AW, NICK...! I WAS MOTIVATIN' YOU. WORKED, DIDN'T IT? INCLINED PRESS...THAT WEIGHT...GOTTA BE A RECORD--

--FOR OUR AGE, I MEAN.

YEAH--

--THAT'S A LITTLE QUALIFICATION BECOMIN' WAY TOO FAMILIAR.

C'MON YOU OLD WARHORSE, MAYBE THE STEAM'LL COOK A FEW YEARS OFF US.

...SHOULD CONSIDER THE *POSITIVE* SIDE, COLONEL FURY.

WE'RE LOOKING AT *DEAD AGENTS*, HAZELTINE--

--AN ENTIRE *OPERATION*, FROM TECHNICIANS TO THE TEAM LEADER. POSITIVE COMES A LITTLE *HARD* FOR ME.

YOU'RE FORGETTING *THIS*, SIR. THE SMALL PLASTIC DISC LEFT ON TEAM LEADER NANJIWARRA'S CORPSE.

AN' NICK AN' ME ARE ALREADY *FAMILIAR* WITH THAT, HAZELTINE, IT'S--

A ZODIAC SYMBOL, *SCORPIO*, OF COURSE, SPECIAL DIRECTOR DUGAN. AVAILABLE ANYWHERE ON CHEAP KEY CHAINS OR AS PRIZES IN BUBBLE GUM MACHINES.

BUT IT'S ALSO THE FIRST *SIGNIFICANT CLUE* TO COME OUR WAY SINCE WE MOUNTED OUR COUNTEROFFENSIVE AGAINST THE TERRORIST SUPPORT NETWORK *SWIFT SWORD*.

OBVIOUSLY THE OBJECT *ITSELF* IS TOO COMMON TO BE TRACED. BUT THE *SYMBOL*, COLONEL--

PERSONALLY. GOOD EXIT LINE, BAD DECISION. SURE, FURY REASONED AS HE STORMED FROM *SHIELD* HEADQUARTERS, IT FIT HIS STYLE. TOUGH LEADER, ALWAYS READY TO SHOW THE TROOPS HOW IT'S DONE,

EXCEPT THAT WASN'T WHY HE WAS DOING IT. HE WOULDN'T BE THIS ANGRY, THIS FED UP WITH AN OVEREAGER WETNOSE LIKE HAZEL-TINE. NO, STYLE DIDN'T ENTER INTO IT...

...MOTIVE DID. AND UNTIL THIS ENDED-- ONE WAY OR ANOTHER-- HE'D NEVER BE *CERTAIN* OF THAT.

YOU'RE *SCARED,* AND IT MAKES YOU FEEL MORE LIKE AN *OLD MAN* THAN A *MILLION* BENCH PRESSES EVER COULD.

IT'S NOT *HIM,* DAMMIT! YOU *BURIED* HIM. AND YOU MADE SURE *WHO* YOU BURIED.

MAYBE AFTER A DRINK, YOU'LL *BELIEVE* IT AGAIN.

AH, COLONEL, THE *USUAL?*

YEAH, MARIO, I DON'T NEED ANY *SURPRISES.*

JUST *ANSWERS,* AND THEY WON'T COME FROM OUR COMPUTER FILES. NOT WHEN I'VE KEPT 'EM *INCOMPLETE.*

WAS I DOIN' HIM A `LAST FAVOR--KEEPIN' HIS MEMORY CLEAN--AFTER HE PUT THE *BULLET* IN HIS HEAD?

OR WAS I JUST *AFRAID* TO LET ANYONE ELSE FIND OUT *SCORPIO* WAS MY BROTHER *JAKE?*

OKAY, YOU GOT MY *ATTENTION.* THIS JOINT'S DIM ENOUGH AN' LOUD ENOUGH THAT FLASHIN' THOSE ADAMANTIUM CLAWS DIDN'T GET ANYBODY *ELSE'S*--

--BUT WHATEVER HAPPENED TO JUST SAYIN' *HELLO,* LOGAN?

DAVID NANJIWARRA.

**SNIKT**

ME AN' MY FRIEND'LL BE HAVING A *PRIVATE CHAT,* MARIO. HE LISTENS BETTER WHEN HE HAS SOMETHING TO DO WITH HIS *HANDS.* GIVE HIM A *BEER*--

--AN' ME A FRESH OLIVE.

YOUR ORGANIZATION'S TRYIN' TO KEEP ME *OUT* OF THIS, NICK. CAN'T BE DONE.

HEY, AS WOLVERINE, AS ONE OF THE X-MEN, YOU *KNOW* YOUR SITUATION WITH *ANY* LAW ENFORCE-MENT AGENCY IS OFFICIALLY... *DUBIOUS.*

BULL!

DEPENDIN' ON WHO AN' WHEN YOU ASK, MY *OFFICIAL* SITUATION CAN BE ANYTHING FROM USEFUL FREAK TO MUTANT OUTLAW TO LEGALLY *DEAD!*

WE GO BACK *BEFORE* THE X-MEN, FURY... TO MY DAYS WITH *CANADIAN INTELLIGENCE.*

YOU NEVER *USED* TO LET WHAT'S *OFFICIAL* COME AHEAD OF WHAT'S *RIGHT.*

MAYBE THE *DIFFERENCE* USED TO BE *CLEARER.* FORGET THAT. THE *BOTTOM LINE* HASN'T CHANGED--

--A LOT BETTER TO HAVE YOU *WITH* US THAN BUTTIN' *HEADS* EVERY STEP. C'MON.

I'LL CLEAR IT SO YOU CAN ACCOMPANY OUR INVESTIGATING TEAM.

TEAM...? NOT *YOU?*

NICK, YOU ALWAYS *LEAPED* TO GET FROM BEHIND YOUR DESK INTO THE ACTION.

YEAH. MY *FIRST* INCLINATION. BUT I WANT TO SORT SOME STUFF OUT.

MAYBE THE HEAD OF *S.H.I.E.L.D.* *SHOULDN'T* BE INVOLVED IN ITS OPERATIONS. NOT *PERSONALLY.*

I WANT HIS *KILLER.* ANYTHING *BETWEEN* ME AN' THAT--

--WON'T BE FOR *LONG.*

YOUR DECISION. MINE WAS MADE THE MOMENT I HEARD ABOUT DAVID.

ANDROS. PLEASURE PORT FOR TOURISTS, AND GATEWAY TO HUNDREDS OF SMALLER ISLANDS DOTTING THE AEGEAN SEA BETWEEN GREECE AND TURKEY.

A *YACHT...?* YOU'RE WAITING FOR A REAL, HONEST-TO-GOD *YACHT?* TRACEY, DID YOU *HEAR?*

BLAIR, I SPENT THE MORNING DRIPPING COPPERTONE ALL OVER MY *BOD...* NOT INTO MY *EARS.* I HAVEN'T MISSED A *WORD* HE--*MICHAEL,* ISN'T IT?--SAID.

UH... *MIKEL.* BUT... AH... IN ENGLISH, I GUESS THAT'S MICHAEL, ACTUALLY, I KIND OF LIKE... UH... *MIKE.*

WELL, TRACEY AND I ARE IN ON A *CRUISE SHIP,* MIKE. DENTAL HYGIENISTS... OUR BIG TWO WEEK VACATION, RIGHT? NOT LIKE IT HASN'T BEEN *ROMANTIC* OR ANYTHING, BUT NOT ONLY ARE THE *CABINS* CRAMPED...

...SO ARE THE *OPPORTUNITIES,* IT'D BE SO *NEAT* TO FINALLY MEET A CUTE GUY--

--AND NOT WAKE UP IN THE MORNING WITH *SAND* IN YOUR BIKINI, RIGHT? THIS *YACHT,* MIKE...HOW MANY DOES IT *SLEEP?*

*THERE* YOU ARE, DARLING. I WAS GETTING WORRIED SOMETHING MIGHT HAVE *HAPPENED* TO YOU.

MICKEY!

GUESS *SOME* YACHTS ARE CRAMPED AS OUR *CABIN*, WHO KNEW HE WAS INTO *MATURE?*

YOU GIRLS ARE *TOO SWEET*, ENTERTAINING MICKEY, I KNOW HOW *LIMITED* YOUR TIME MUST BE ON THESE *CRUISES*... WE WON'T TAKE ANOTHER *MOMENT* OF IT.

SO... HE DOESN'T *KNOW* WHAT HE'S *MISSING*, MY GOD, BLAIR--

"--TAKE AWAY THAT MILLION-DOLLAR *CONDITIONING*, SHE'S OLD ENOUGH TO BE HIS *MOTHER.*"

YES, I WAS BITCHY, BECAUSE IN MY PLACE, THAT'S HOW THEY'D BE, THEY'LL GOSSIP A BIT--

--UNTIL SOME *LOCAL ZORBA* GIVES THEM THE "I'LL TEACH YOU THE *REAL WAY* TO DRINK *OZU*" ROUTINE.

THEN WE'LL BE *FORGOTTEN*, MICKEY, WHICH IS *EXACTLY* WHAT WE WANT.

NOW, ARE YOU GOING TO TELL ME HOW IT WENT--

--OR SHOULD I JUST LET YOU *SULK* IN PEACE AND READ THE *OFFICIAL REPORT* AT HOME?

WE'RE ALMOST THERE, AND YOU *KNOW* HOW IT WENT. SAME AS IN TAIWAN, SAME AS IN THE BALKANS--

--MOM.

PERU. ROTORS THUDDING, THE GOVERNMENT HELICOPTER BANKED FOR ITS APPROACH TO MACHU PICCHU. THE THREE S.H.I.E.L.D. AGENTS ABOARD CAME ALERT, TENSED FOR THE JOB AHEAD.

THE FOURTH PASSENGER SHOWED NO REACTION, BUT HIS THOUGHTS WERE RACING, CARRIED BY THE SOUND OF THE ROTORS...

...TO ANOTHER TIME, ANOTHER JOB. AND...

RUNNIN'... RUNNIN' FOR MY LIFE...

"...IN THE DESERT SUN."

BA-DUUM!

TRACKING A TERRORIST ASSASSIN HAD LED LOGAN FROM CANADA TO AUSTRALIA'S TANAMI DESERT, AND THE SECRET TRAINING CAMP FROM WHICH HIS MAN HAD GRADUATED.

HITTING THE CAMP WENT WELL, ONLY HIS SWIFTLY IMPROVISED DESTRUCTION...

...DIDN'T CATCH EVERYONE.

SO LOGAN RAN FOR HIS LIFE IN THE DESERT SUN...

...IN VAIN.

THEY LEFT HIM FOR DEAD, WHICH HE SHOULD HAVE BEEN.

EXCEPT HE WAS A MUTANT, WITH THE MUTANT ABILITY TO HEAL HIMSELF. HE JUST NEEDED TIME, AND WATER, SO HE DIDN'T FRY FIRST FROM DEHYDRATION.

JUST WATER, WHICH HE DIDN'T HAVE.

GOTTA... KEEP M-MOVIN' ...MAYBE... CATCH SCENT... F-FIND...

...NOTHIN'...

FINE PLACE TO GO WALKABOUT.

INTELLIGENCE SERVICES IN AMERICA HIRE A LOT OF MADMEN, DO THEY?

I'M... CANADIAN, N-NOT

POOR BLOODY EXCUSE, PARTICULARLY AFTER THE MESS YOU MADE OF MY FIRST UNDER-COVER ASSIGNMENT.

DAVID NANJIWARRA, WITH THE ASIO. SORT OF YOUR DOWNUNDER CIA. THEY GOT WORD IN YOU WERE ABOUT.

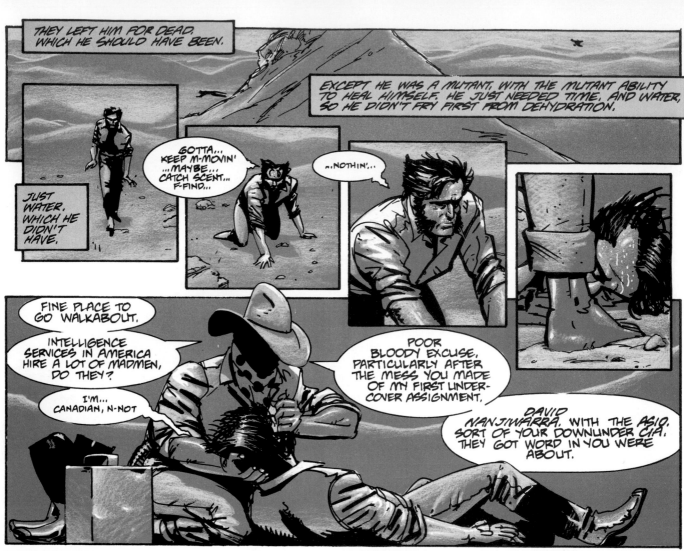

I WAS THERE AS A LABORER. ONE MORE ABO TO THE LOT. WHATEVER THEIR POLI-TICS...THEY STILL TEND TO TYPECAST, BIT LIKE MY SUPERIORS, ACTUALLY.

AND JUST AS I WAS MAKING PROGRESS, YOU PUT PAID TO IT ALL... MY HIDDEN SHORT WAVE INCLUDED.

SO MUCH FOR CALLING FOR HELP.

ONLY WAY OUT IS TO LEG IT, OR DIE. YOUR CONDITION, THERE MAY NOT BE A DIFFERENCE.

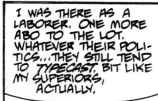

JUST...GET ME STARTED! WE'LL TAKE THE REST... AS IT COMES...

TOO LUCKY! A CANADIAN! A MADMAN... AND FEISTY!

THEY WALKED. LONG, BRUTAL DAYS, ENDLESS, AGONIZING MILES, IMPOSSIBLE MILES...

...EXCEPT FOR DAVID NANJIWARRA AND HIS KNOW-LEDGE OF THE UNFORGIVING LANDSCAPE.

YOU'D ALREADY HAVE... BEATEN THIS FURNACE... IF NOT FOR ME. LEAVES A LOT... T'PAY BACK. MORE THAN I CAN EVER...

NO WORRIES. 'BOUT NOW, LOGAN... I'D SETTLE FOR A BEER... LAGER... ICE COLD...

IT BECAME A RUNNING JOKE IN THEIR WALK THROUGH HELL. IT BONDED THEM, KEPT THEM GOING, UNTIL...

JUST LIKE CIVILIZATION.

TWO BEERS...? ONLY IF YOU'RE DRINKIN' 'EM Y'RSELF, SPORT. DON'T SERVE ABOS...FOR THEIR OWN GOOD, Y'UNDERSTAN'.

I UNDERSTAND YOU LOOKED ME IN THE EYE AND MADE THE BIGGEST MISTAKE IN AN OBVIOUSLY MISERABLE LIFE. LOOK AGAIN, "SPORT." NOW--

LAST CHANCE. TWO LAGERS. ICE COLD. ONE FOR ME, ONE FOR MY FRIEND. FOR YOUR OWN GOOD.

THE BEERS COULD HAVE BEEN COLDER, BUT THEY WERE COLD ENOUGH FOR A BUSH OUTPOST PERCHED ON THE RUMP OF NOWHERE. COLD ENOUGH AND GOOD ENOUGH...

...THEY PROVED EVEN HELL HAD ITS LIMITS.

...TO KEEP THEM DRINKING. AND TALKING. SILLY, AT FIRST. IN TIME... SERIOUSLY.

...LIFE WASN'T MEANT TO BE EASY, THE SAYING GOES AROUND HERE, LOGAN. IF YOU'RE ABORIGINE, IT SEEMS TO GO DOUBLE. OR HAS IN MY SITUATION...

AUSTRALIA'S GOT NO LOCK AND KEY ON PREJUDICE. BUT IF THAT'S THE PROBLEM, DAVID. I'VE HEARD ABOUT A NEW OUTFIT. AN INTERNATIONAL ONE. OUGHT TO AVOID THAT KINDA THING.

THEY CALL IT SHIELD. WHO KNOWS--

"...WHERE IT COULD LEAD?"

CHECKED THE LAST OF THE BODY BAGS. GUESS WE CAN SHIP 'EM HOME NOW, HUH, WOLVERINE? WOLVERINE?

WOLVERINE...? YOU OKAY...?

JUST THINKIN'--

THINKIN' ABOUT HAVIN' A BEER.

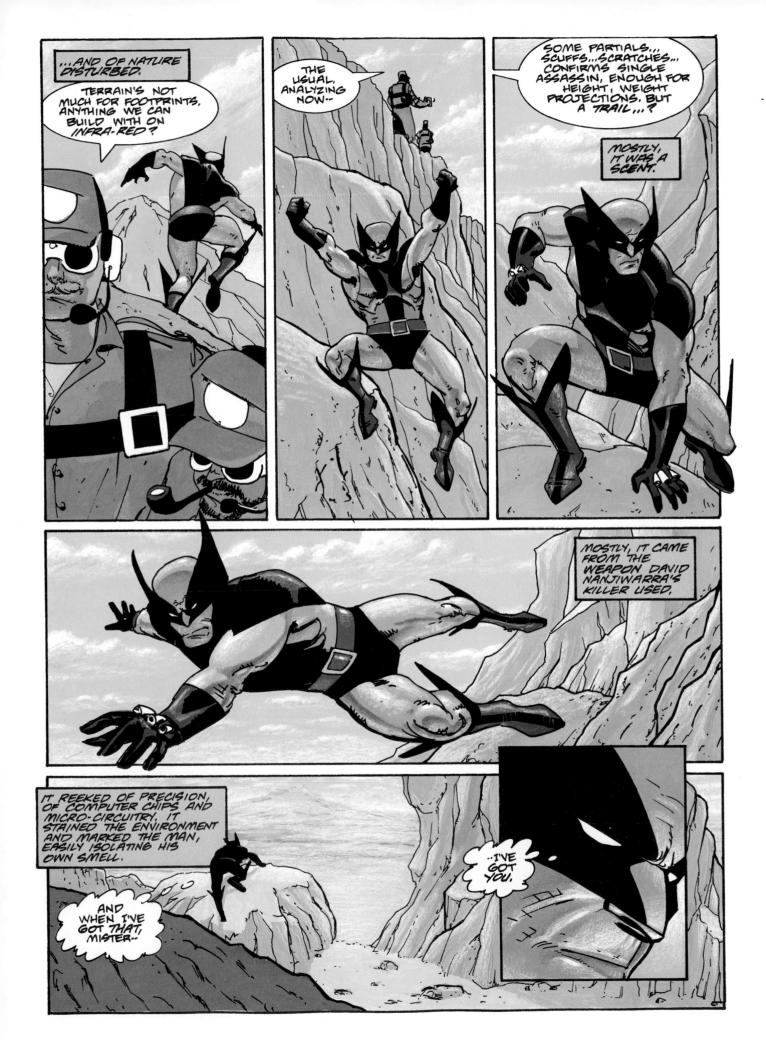

IF HE FOLLOWED FAR ENOUGH, THE LONG TRAIL WALKED BY THE ASSASSIN ENDED MILES FROM MACHU PICCHU...

...AT A LOCAL COPPER MINE.

PRIVATE AIRSTRIP... WELL MAINTAINED, BETTER THAN MOST OF THE MINING EQUIPMENT I PASSED SNEAKIN' IN...

AND THE FIELD'S OPERATIONS HUT APPEARED PARTICULARLY WELL-GUARDED, UNTIL...

QUE ES ESTE?!

EL AVION...! FUEGO! FUEGO!

RIGHT, LET'S SEE IF THE GUNS AND MUSCLE ARE REALLY PROTECTING OLD FLIGHT PLANS.

THEY MUST COME CHEAPER HERE THAN GOOD LOCKS FOR THE FILES.

OR A FIRST-RATE CODE SYSTEM!

PLACE IS A FRONT FOR SWIFT SWORD! PART OF THEIR ARMS SMUGGLING NETWORK.

YOU WERE CLOSER THAN YOU KNEW, DAVID. AND THEY BROUGHT IN THE HIRED GUN TO SEE YOU NEVER GOT CLOSER.

ZDOWWW!

SANTA MADRE! H-HOW...?!

OOOCAOOOOCAOOOOCAOOOO

ALARM'S FROM THE OPS ROOM! BUT--

--SECURITY SEALS ARE STILL INTACT!

BLOW THE DAMN DOORS AN' FIGURE IT OUT LATER!

HE SAVED THEM THE TROUBLE.

SHDAAAK!

THE ROOFTOP WAS THE CLOSEST ESCAPE, AND THESE GUARDS WOULDN'T LIVE TO--

SONAR PHANTOMS GENERATED BY HIS WEAPON'S CIRCUITRY HAD DISGUISED HIS SCALING OF THE BUILDING'S OUTSIDE WALL...

...BUT ONCE HE BLASTED INSIDE, THE TIME FOR ANY FURTHER SUBTLETIES WERE PAST.

WHO ARE YOU ?!

WHO IN HELL ARE

SPLASH!

IMPACT DIDN'T QUITE... FINISH YOU, OLD MAN...?

STILL WITH ME...? STILL WANT... ANSWERS...?

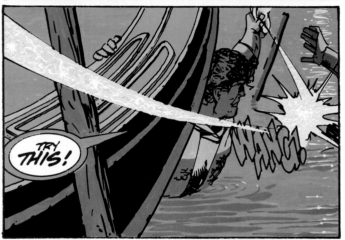

TRY THIS!

I'M JACOB FURY'S SON! YOUR BROTHER JAKE!

THE BROTHER YOU MURDERED! LIKE I'M GOING TO MURDER YOU!

IF ONLY IT COULD BE NOW. BUT NO, NOT WITH S.H.I.E.L.D. AGENTS SWARMING IN. NOT WITH CANAL SLUDGE FOULING HIS WEAPON'S DELICATE CIRCUITRY.

NEXT TIME, MIKEL FURY THOUGHT.

NEXT TIME!

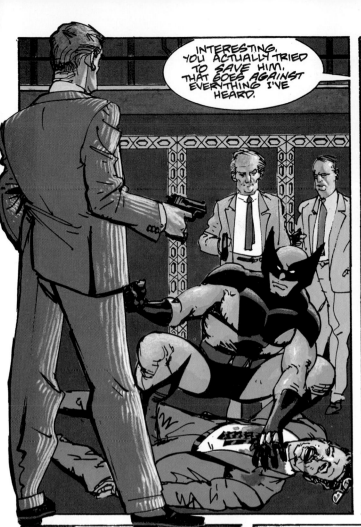

INTERESTING, YOU ACTUALLY TRIED TO *SAVE* HIM, THAT GOES AGAINST *EVERYTHING* I'VE HEARD.

PERHAPS THE FAMOUS *WOLVERINE* ISN'T SUCH AN *ANIMAL* AFTER ALL.

I'M *AMBER D'ALEXIS.* I RUN THIS *ESTABLISHMENT,* AND AID *THESE GENTLEMEN...* ALL MEMBERS IN *GOOD STANDING* OF *SWIFT SWORD.*

WHEN THEY DECIDED THEIR *PERUVIAN* OPERATION WAS NO LONGER *EFFECTIVE,* I SUGGESTED SACRIFICING IT AS *BAIT* FOR A *TRAP..*

--WHICH SHOULD HAVE LURED *S.H.I.E.L.D.'S* DIRECTOR, *NICK FURY,* OR SOME OF HIS *TOP AGENTS.*

NO OFFENSE, BUT *YOU'LL* HAVE TO DO.

YES, I WILL, LADY, WHAT I DO *BEST.*

SNIKT!

SNIKT!

THEY WERE GOOD. DEDICATED. SWIFT SWORD WAS A SUPPORT NETWORK FOR A NUMBER OF CAUSES, AFTER ALL. MOST FAVORED SOCIAL CHANGE FROM THE BARREL OF A GUN...

...OR THE EXPLOSION OF A WELL-PLACED BOMB...

...OR WHATEVER DEATH AND DESTRUCTION IT TOOK.

THEY WERE GOOD. DEDICATED. AND IT WASN'T NEARLY ENOUGH.

TRAPS CAN WORK TWO WAYS, LADY.

WONDER ABOUT THE ANIMAL IN ME? IT'S COMIN' AT YOU! FOR DAVID NANJIWARRA AND--

NO!

NOBODY HURTS MY PARENTS! NOBODY!

THIS IS ABOUT PERU! YOUR FIGHT'S WITH ME--

--THIS SHOULD HAVE BEEN *NICK FURY.*

YOU'LL HAVE TO DO.

THROUGH PAIN AND SEMI-CONSCIOUSNESS, LOGAN TRIED TO RISE BEFORE THE KILLING BLAST.

THEN...

...THE LIGHTS WENT OUT.

DARKNESS, SO TOTAL IT MIGHT WELL HAVE BEEN DEATH...

...UNTIL SOMETHING JERKED HIM VIOLENTLY UPRIGHT!

.......

W-WHAT...?

I SAID, IF YOU'RE GONNA DEPEND ON OTHER PEOPLE TO HAUL YOUR BUTT OUT OF *TROUBLE* --

-- TRADE IN THAT ADAMANTIUM SKELETON FOR SOMETHING LIGHTER.

NICK...! HOW...!

BLACKLIGHT BOMB.

UNLESS SOMEBODY'S WEARING INFRA-RED CONTACT LENSES... THE EFFECT'LL COVER US LONG ENOUGH TO GET AWAY.

"...ON UNDERCOVER ASSIGNMENT.

"I WAS PLAYING SHADY CITIZEN. A GROWTH INDUSTRY BACK IN MACAO. UP THERE WITH TOURISM AND TEXTILES.

"MADE ME OKAY IN THE RIGHT PLACES. LIKE THE CLUB WE SUSPECTED SERVED AS CLEARING HOUSE FOR AN ESPIONAGE RING WE WERE OUT TO BREAK.

"ALL I HAD TO DO WAS GET ENOUGH PROOF TO MAKE THE LOCAL AUTHORITIES ACT ON OUR SUSPICIONS.

"MOSTLY, THAT MEANT I DID A LOT OF WATCHING...

"...A LITTLE GAMBLING...

"...AND TRIED TO CULTIVATE THE MANAGEMENT."

I'M AFRAID YOU LOSE, AGAIN.

YOU MAKE IT PRETTY PAINLESS. I'M SURPRISED THEY DON'T HAVE YOU WORK A TABLE MORE OFTEN.

I ONLY DO IT TO KEEP MY HAND IN...OR MEET CUSTOMERS THAT INTRIGUE ME.

AMBER D'ALEXIS. IT'S MY CLUB.

"AMBER D'ALEXIS. HER LIFE STORY VARIED, DEPENDING ON WHOSE INTELLIGENCE FILES YOU SAW. BUT SEE ENOUGH OF THEM, YOU'D FIND SOME CONSISTENCIES.

"HER PARENTS WERE EUROPEAN. SETTLED IN ASIA, DIED WHEN SHE WAS A KID. SHE GREW UP ON THE STREETS, SURVIVING ANY WAY IT TOOK.

"BECAME HER POLITICS, REALLY. SURVIVING. SURVIVING WELL. IF LIVES WERE LOST OR GOVERNMENTS FELL AS A RESULT OF WHAT SHE DID TO SURVIVE...

"...WELL, LIVES WERE LOST AND GOVERNMENTS FELL ANYWAY. MEANTIME, SHE HAD HOLDINGS TO LOOK AFTER.

DIMENSION RESEARCH →

"SOME OF THEM WERE LEGITIMATE. PLACES TO LAUNDER HER SHARE OF THE SPY MONEY PASSING BACK AND FORTH ON HER GAMING TABLES DISGUISED AS BETS.

"ONE IN PARTICULAR, A BIOPHYSICS DEVELOPMENT FIRM, DREW HER ATTENTION...

"...AND GAVE ME AN EYEFUL WHEN I DISCOVERED WHY.

"MAYBE TO PROTECT HER INVESTMENTS, MAYBE 'CAUSE SHE PREFERRED TO PLAY OUTSIDE HER CASINO, AMBER HAD A THING WITH ONE OF THE RESEARCH GUYS...

"...WHO TURNED OUT TO BY MY KID BROTHER, JAKE FURY.

"WHO TURNED OUT TO BE IN LOVE,"

"...A *MISTAKE* WITH AMBER? NICK, I CAME HERE ON THE QUIET TO *ESCAPE* THIS BIG BROTHER CRAP... TO GET A LIFE *BEYOND* YOUR SHADOW.

WHO *NEEDS* YOU SHOWING UP FROM NOWHERE WITH YOUR *CERTIFIED WAR HERO* ADVICE?

"SO, INSTEAD... I GAVE THEM MY *BLESSING.*

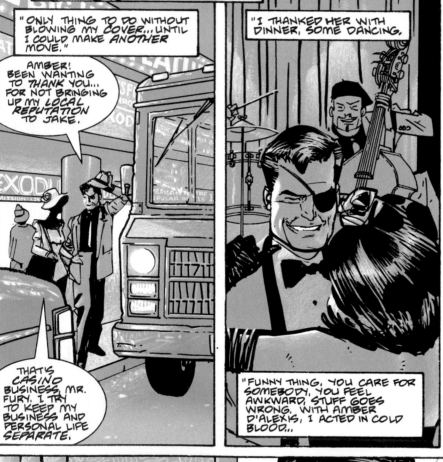

"ONLY THING TO DO WITHOUT BLOWING MY *COVER*...UNTIL I COULD MAKE *ANOTHER* MOVE."

AMBER! BEEN WANTING TO *THANK* YOU... FOR NOT BRINGING UP MY *LOCAL REPUTATION* TO JAKE.

THAT'S *CASINO* BUSINESS, MR. FURY. I TRY TO KEEP MY BUSINESS AND PERSONAL LIFE *SEPARATE.*

"I *THANKED* HER WITH DINNER, SOME DANCING,

"FUNNY THING, YOU CARE FOR SOMEBODY, YOU FEEL AWKWARD, STUFF GOES WRONG, WITH AMBER D'ALEXIS, I ACTED IN COLD BLOOD...

"...AND THE *HEAT* WAS THERE FROM THE START. MAYBE YEARS OF USING *OTHERS* MADE HER INSENSITIVE TO *BEING USED.* WHATEVER THE REASON, IT WORKED. WORKED *WELL.*

"SHE FORGOT JAKE, AND BUSINESS,

"I *DIDN'T.*

"NO MORE THAN I FORGOT THE *EXPRESSION* ON HER FACE WHEN IT *ENDED*...WHEN I HAD THE *EVIDENCE* I NEEDED FOR THE MACAO AUTHORITIES... WHEN I HAD THE *TRUTH* I NEEDED FOR JAKE ABOUT THE KIND OF WOMAN HE LOVED.

SO? YOU CAN'T *ERASE* THE PAST, NICK. YOU CAN'T EVEN *FIX* IT...YOUR LITTLE BROTHER MADE *CERTAIN* OF THAT.

THERE'S STILL HIS *BOY,* LOGAN.

NO, THERE'S STILL A *KILLER.* ANY *DOUBTS*...YOU'RE *WAY* OUT OF LINE ACTIN' ALONE.

IT'S NOT THAT *SIMPLE.* TO HIT OUR ANTI-TERRORIST OPERATIONS SO HARD, THAT KID HAS TO HAVE *INSIDE* INFORMATION.

MEANS A *LEAK* WITHIN *S.H.I.E.L.D.*... MAYBE EVEN A *TRAITOR.* AND *JUSTIFICATION* FOR MY PLAYIN' THIS SOLO. BUT I'M *STILL*--

--LOGAN, HOW DO YOU DO THIS?

YOU *QUIT,* NICK. LET *ME* FIND SCORPIO.

NO, HOW DO YOU *EAT* THIS STUFF WITHOUT UTENSILS?

SORRY, BUT SCORPIO'S *MY* PROBLEM. I'VE GOTTA FACE IT. HAULIN' YOU FROM AMBER'S CLUB, I ALSO MANAGED TO SLIP A *HOMING TRACER* ONTO THE KID. SHOULD LEAD ME--

BETTER LEAD *US,* NICK, COMES THE *CRUNCH,* IF YOU *CAN'T* DO WHAT HAS TO BE DONE--

SNK

--I *CAN.*

--AT LEAST THIS *TRACKING UNIT* DOES. PINPOINTS OUR *TRACER* READINGS TO THERE.

NIFTY VILLA. AMBER'S STYLE ALL RIGHT.

PROBABLY EXPLAINS WHY THEY DON'T GET DOWN TO THE *RUINS*, SPREAD *FRESH SCENTS* LIKE THEY SHOULD. WHAT DO YOU THINK?

I THINK IT LOOKS ENOUGH LIKE A *FORTRESS*. YOU COULD BE RIGHT.

BALCONY ON THE *SEAWARD* SIDE, SOME GARAGE-LIKE ENTRANCE UP THE TRAIL. CALL IT.

BALCONY. TRAIL LOOKS STEEP FOR A MAN MY *AGE*.

FACT THAT MY CLAWS WILL WORK BEST AGAINST THESE *IRON SHUTTERS* HAS NOTHIN' TO DO WITH IT, RIGHT?

HOWEVER YOUR *EMOTIONS* ARE TWISTED IN ALL THIS, FURY--

"--AT LEAST YOU'RE STILL MAKING *DECISIONS* LIKE A *TOP KICK*."

PLACED *CIRCUIT DISRUPTOR*... IT'LL HANDLE *ALARMS* AN' *SENSORS*.

AMBER.... MIKEL....

"...NOW WE SEE IF *I* CAN HANDLE YOU."

FAINTLY, DEEP WITHIN THE HOUSE, THERE WAS MUSIC, VOICES.

FURY RUSHED TOWARD THE SOUND, KNOWING WOLVERINE WOULD BE RUSHING AS WELL.

SCARED IF HE GETS TO 'EM *FIRST*? WHO'D YOU BLAB ABOUT THE *TRACER*?

NO, YOU WANTED LOGAN, FELT YOU MIGHT *NEED* HIM...TO KEEP YOU HONEST.

THE SONG WAS CLEAR AS HE HIT THE DOOR. OLD COLE PORTER, RODGERS AND HART, MAYBE. ONE HE'D DANCED TO...

...IN MACAO.

NICHOLAS...! WHAT A *NICE* SURPRISE!

SORRY I CAN'T BE THERE *IN PERSON* TO SHARE IT. WELCOME TO MY *MEDIA ROOM*.

HOPE YOU *APPROVE*. OVER THE YEARS, MY SON'S HAD QUITE AN *EDUCATION* HERE, ABOUT YOU...AND JAKE.

LOOKING FOR YOUR *TRACER*..? ON THE STEREO, TOO, NICHOLAS... IT'S BEEN ON *CONTINUOUS PLAY* SINCE WE LEFT. THOSE OLD TAPES ARE SO HARD TO REPLACE, BESIDES--

*AMBER!* YOU--

--WHY MISS A *WORD* OF THIS PRE-RECORDED LITTLE VIDEO YOU *TRIGGERED* BY OPENING THE DOOR?

IT'S ONE OF THE *LAST THINGS* YOU'LL EVER HEAR.

FROM THE HOTEL ATRIUM WHERE MIKEL HAD LED FURY AND WOLVERINE, IT WAS FOURTEEN STORIES TO THE ROOF.

SH-DOW!

FOURTEEN STORIES...

...AND ONE BLAST OF THE SCORPIO KEY.

I KNEW THINGS HAD GONE WRONG WHEN THE TRACKING UNIT PINPOINTED YOU HEADED HERE, MICKEY..

--BUT WOLVERINE IS A PROBLEM I THOUGHT WE'D ALREADY SOLVED!

NOT TO WORRY, BABY WE BEAT HIM ONCE, WE WON'T LOSE NOW..

--JUST KEEP THE STUBBORN LITTLE BEAST OCCUPIED.

LEAVE THE REST TO MOMMA--

..AND THE TURBOPROPS!

BUT THERE WAS MORE THAN ONE UNSOLVED PROBLEM FOR AMBER D'ALEXIS.

NICK FURY. LETTING S.H.I.E.L.D. TECHNOLOGY...

VROOOOOOOSHH

...MAKE UP WHERE HIS TIRING BODY FAILED.

KRA-DAASH

WOLVERINE! I'VE STOPPED THE PLANE!

MIKEL--

"..I'VE STOPPED YOUR MOTHER, TOO! THERE'S NO GETTING ME WITHOUT GOING THROUGH HER.

DON'T MAKE ME CHOOSE BETWEEN A FRIEND AND MY BROTHER'S SON.

YOU DON'T WANT THAT, KID. GIVE IT UP!

YOU, TOO, LOGAN!

HE CAN'T, NICHOLAS--

YOU WON'T *LIVE* TO FIND OUT!

I DON'T *NEED* THE *SCORPIO KEY* TO *FINISH* YOU!

*NO!* LOGAN! MIKEL!...

"...ISN'T JAKE'S SON, HE'S YOURS!" THE WORDS HAMMERED IN NICK FURY'S MIND. OVER AND OVER.

HAD TO BE A LIE, RIGHT? A FINAL CRAZY TRICK FROM A REVENGE-CRAZY LADY. HAD TO BE, RIGHT?

WHAT IF IT WASN'T? WHAT IF THAT WAS HIS SON TRYING TO FORCE WOLVERINE OFF THE ROOF...

...WHILE LOGAN TRIED TO GUT HIM STEM TO STERN IN MEMORY OF DAVID NANJIWARRA?

IT STILL CAME DOWN TO A CHOICE.

HARDER TO MAKE.

IMPOSSIBLE TO AVOID.

P-KOW!

—FINISHED HIM, NICHOLAS, WHICH BRINGS US BACK TO YOU.

THE BOY NEEDS MEDICAL ATTENTION. WITH ALL THE S.H.I.E.L.D. AND S.W.A.T. TEAM 'COPTERS BUZZIN' AROUND NOW, WE CAN--

STOP IT.

DON'T TRY TO PLAY ON MY CONCERN. I SACRIFICED MICKEY YEARS AGO. AND ONCE YOU'RE DEAD--

--HE HAS NO LIFE ANYWAY.

THIS WILL BE AN ACT OF MERCY FOR HIM, AND AS PAINFUL AS I CAN MAKE IT FOR YOU, NICHOLAS. SOUND COLD...? WELL, COLD NEVER HURT ME!

RELAXING FOR ONE INSTANT AND LOVING DID! YOU AND MACAO, NICHOLAS...PAIN I NEVER GOT OVER, PAIN I CAN NEVER MAKE UP.

BUT WATCHING YOU DIE IS A START...; AND WATCHING YOU DIE WITH THE SON YOU'LL NEVER KNOW IS BETTER YET!

DIE FOR ME, NICHOLAS!

M--MOM...?

IT MIGHT HAVE BEEN A WARNING.

OR A CRY OF DISBELIEF.

LOGAN WOULD NEVER BE SURE.

NO MORE THAN HE'D EVER BE SURE IF THE WOMAN STARTING TO TURN CAUSED A WOUNDING THRUST TO BECOME A KILLING STROKE...

...OR IF THE BERSERKER DEEP WITHIN HIM DEMANDED IT ANYWAY.

IN ANY EVENT...

...THE PAIN AND HATE DRIVING AMBER D'ALEXIS WAS STILLED.

BUT...

HER KID...! ESCAPING!

MOVING, BUT WITH ALL HE'S SEEN AN' HEARD--

..GOTTA STILL BE IN SHOCK. MY RESPONSIBILITY NOW, WOLVERINE. STAY OUT OF IT!

TILL HE STARTS KILLING AGAIN?

NICK, THE LADY'S BENT HIS MIND WAY PAST UNTWISTING!

SNIPER TEAMS ARE GETTIN' ANTSY. WHAT'S THE TARGET SITUATION?

OUR TWO WHITE HATS ARE FINALLY IN THE CLEAR... BUT FIGHTIN' WITH EACH OTHER.

TELL ALL TEAMS TO EYEBALL THAT V.T.O.L.! BAD GUY'S USIN' IT FOR COVER AN~

THE FIRST THING NICK FURY HEARD AFTER DISCOVERING HE'D SURVIVED WAS...

...WOLVERINE!

INTERESTING SITUATION, SONNY--

THE HOTEL MALL HAD BEEN CLEARED WHEN THE ROOFTOP FIGHT BEGAN. NOW IT WAS FILLED WITH S.H.I.E.L.D. AGENTS, LOCAL LAW OFFICERS...

...AND A SENSE OF IMPENDING DEATH.

--I SPRING MY CLAWS, YOU DIE OF A HEADACHE, GUARANTEED. 'COURSE, YOUR DEATH SPASM CAN TRIGGER THAT KEY DINGUS... LEAVE ME WITHOUT A HEAD.

SAME IF YOU ACT FIRST. BASIC STALEMATE--

--UNTIL I GET SO MAD I FORGET THAT AND ONLY REMEMBER YOU'RE DAVID NANJIWARRA'S KILLER.

LOGAN--

--YOU CAN BACK DOWN.

WHY? BECAUSE OF HIM? YOU CAN'T THINK OF MIKEL AS YOUR SON, NICK, HE'S AMBERS MACHINE... A LIVING PIECE OF REVENGE.

BECAUSE OF DAVID NANJIWARRA.

REMEMBER I FIGURED SOMEONE INSIDE S.H.I.E.L.D. WAS FEEDING INFO TO SWIFT SWORD FOR SCORPIO'S ATTACKS?

I CHECKED THE MASTER COMPUTER SOON AS WE GOT HERE. ONLY ONE AGENT IN OUR ANTI-TERRORIST OPERATION SERVED IN ALL THE PLACES MIKEL HIT--

--YOUR FRIEND, DAVID.

NANJIWARRA WAS PASSED OVER FOR PROMOTION ONCE. LATER, HIS SUPERVISOR WAS FOUND TO BE PREJUDICED. WE RECTIFIED THE INCIDENT--

WAS ~BUT THE *DAMAGE* HAD TO PLAY ON HIS *FRUSTRATION* AT FINDING PREJUDICE EVERY-WHERE AND *TURN* HIM. AND WHEN THEY HAD ALL THEY *NEEDED~*

~HE WAS SET UP TO *DIE* IN PERU. THEY TOOK WHAT DAVID WAS AND *TWISTED* IT, LOGAN, JUST LIKE~

YEAH~

~JUST LIKE~

~AMBER AND *THIS* KID.

OKAY, NICK~

~HE'S *YOURS.*

BUT THE *SCORPIO KEY...*

...WAS STILL AIMED AND PRIMED...

...ALONG WITH *EVERY* OTHER WEAPON IN THE ATRIUM MALL.

YOU'RE *HURT* SON, MORE WAYS THAN THAT *SHOULDER.* WHATEVER'S KICKIN' AROUND IN YOUR *MIND...* DOESN'T HAVE TO BE DECIDED *NOW,* UNDERSTAND?

MIKE! MIKE? YOU DON'T HAVE TO *DECIDE,* YOU.

THE KEY WAVERED...~

...AND FELL, CLATTERING *LOUDLY* IN THE SURROUND-ING SILENCE.

WOUNDS *PROBABLY* GOT TO 'IM. BUT MAYBE *I* DID. HOW WOULD YOU CALL IT?

I'D SAY YOU'VE *STILL* GOT A *STALE-MATE.*

YEAH. WELL... *SOMETIMES* THAT'S A *STARTING POINT.*